W0259796

SUNRISE IN THE EYES OF THE SNOWMAN

ALSO BY GORAN SIMIĆ

POETRY

From Sarajevo with Sorrow (Biblioasis, 2005)

Immigrant Blues (Brick Books, 2003)

STORIES

Looking for Tito (Frog Hollow Press, 2010)

Yesterday's People (Biblioasis, 2005)

SUNRISE IN THE EYES OF THE SNOWMAN

SUNRISE IN THE EYES OF THE SNOWMAN

GORAN SIMIĆ

POEMS

BIBLIOASIS

FIRST EDITION

Library and Archives Canada Cataloguing in Publication

Simić, Goran, 1952-
Sunrise in the eyes of the snowman / Goran Simić.

Poems.
ISBN 978-1-897231-93-7

I. Title.

PS8587.I3119S86 2010 C811'.54 C2010-904597-1

Edited by Zachariah Wells

Canada Council for the Arts Conseil des Arts du Canada

Canadian Heritage Patrimoine canadien

ONTARIO ARTS COUNCIL
CONSEIL DES ARTS DE L'ONTARIO

Biblioasis acknowledges the ongoing financial support of the Government of Canada through The Canada Council for the Arts, Canadian Heritage, the Book Publishing Industry Development Program (BPIDP); and the Government of Ontario through the Ontario Arts Council.

PRINTED AND BOUND IN CANADA

CONTENTS

to the Snowlady

Sunrise in the Eyes of the Snowman

Kiss me. Breathe into my mouth the way lovers do.
Taste my neck before I melt down to my waist.
Kiss me when only shiny flakes are left.

When horoscopes start sounding like weather reports,
when the radio announces short sleeves on spring uniforms,
let me love myself hugging ice cubes in the bottom of your glass.

Every morning gives birth to the night,
the time when your guests come dressed in black.
I repeat your words engraved on my wedding ring:
flowers are replaceable and only flower pots remain.

But will you love me, a swollen carrot
and two charcoal eyes on the pavement
in a cold puddle?

WALKING BACKWARD

What I Was Told

When I was born everybody rejoiced.
This is what I was told.
I was also told that in his notes my father the King
described hundreds of tents in front of the castle
for the common people's celebration of my birth.
For months wine flowed and roasted quail were eaten
until the wine started to sour
and quail started smelling of wine.

My father the King invited the best fortune tellers in the country
to read my kingdom's fate from my baby palm.
Some of them were richly rewarded.
No trace of the unfortunate others was found in my father's notes.

When I grew tall enough to touch my father's shield,
he issued a state decree ordering
the people of our kingdom to build a castle for me
on the hill. I could smell the sweat
of those who pulled stone slabs up the slope
while I lolled on my throne.

Those who survived the ten years of work
are mentioned in my father's notes. This is what I was told.
Those who didn't were buried in the castle's foundation
and were not recorded in my father's notes.

I forgot the name of my bride.
The taste of matrimonial wine lasted no longer
than the wedding night
when I had to lead my army to war with our neighbours.
My father told me to follow the tradition
and that I will find reasons once I learn how to read.

Sitting on my black horse, watching graves being dug in our wake,
I wondered why people called my army the Virus of Death,

why the sunset scares me
even after the leaves under my horse's hooves
changed colours ten times.

Once my sword acquired the scent of burnt homes and rotting
flesh,
I returned to my kingdom in a golden carriage.
But when I arrived
nobody was there to decorate my exhausted soldiers with garlands.
Only wretched old men and witches were begging forgiveness
for failing to predict my return.
The plague had eaten my father the King,
and my darling whose name I lost in the roll call of my generals.

All I had left from my kingdom were neglected fields
and a notebook that I couldn't read.

Now I sit in my tower with a crown on my head.
I watch storks leaving the cold chimneys of my kingdom,
while I listen to the wind riffling the sheets of my empty bed,
leafing through the pages of my father's notebook.

In this very moment I would happily exchange
my glory and my golden crown,
for someone who would teach me to read.

I Am Just a Title

When my blood goes to sleep and my eyes turn to dust
When I feel the wind on my neck and catch fever,
I'll let my iron hands embrace the rust
and say I'm a drop in what once was a river.

Once my cane becomes my better half and my heart defers to the
    cane,
dried flowers smell like skin and old photos like fresh flowers,
I'll curse my passport's stamps: so many crossings in vain
seeking my faces buried deep in my lovers.

At the end of this road to the land I won't reach
the angel will sing: You're too small to do something bigger.
Oh, Goran, why did you cheat me, drinking wine spiked with
    bleach?
I don't know. Let me smile. He's coming, my friend the
    gravedigger.

Walking Backwards

Be humble, I was told, when facing the history books.
Let the museums instruct you that crime can be fair.
Learn of lures that conceal a hundred golden hooks.
Feel guilty at crime scenes even if you weren't there—

when soldiers were ordered not to reason why;
when truth was a victim and medals shone like swords;
when blood lived in poems and love turned to a cry
behind lines of barbed wire. I lived in a no-man's world

where a rusted sun pretended to know the matter,
when mirrors reflected nothing but pictures of the dead.
Had condoms not been invented, would history look better
had a production line for soldiers made mattresses instead?

Where do I go from now when now seems like my past,
toothlessly singing the anthem, that soil-indulgent song?
When I asked the old frames to embrace me freshly cast,
I was walking backwards. And I was dead wrong.

A Former School Beauty Cries in the Basement

At school,
you were never taught to knock on a door
behind which someone is crying.

A spider crawls across her nightgown,
the pencil she once offered to strangers, should they wish
to capture her beauty, lies idly on a stack of letters
from which the stamps have escaped.

The light coming from the eyes of mice,
twinkling behind the old clock,
seems to be the only light still shining.

It appears as if she is praying.

A former school beauty sobs in the basement
like some child crying at the base of a pyramid
and I can no longer bear the chameleons
that do not want to climb down from my forehead,
nor taste the opium on my lips when I get my paycheque
so that a few days later I might spell like a pupil:

the dog adopts his master's face
and the master adopts his dog's.

I know that it's her head that burns in the blaze,
that a pillow smoulders in the empty crib.

All those books about great love affairs
I once loaned her
now resemble old coffins
because my love never settled in her stomach,
because the pages of those books flew off
with a flock of butterflies.

The only thing that remains is my sorrow,
a butterfly mesh.

Adam

They tell me I'll be grown when I fit
grandpa's shoes and can tell my sister's pubic hair from my own.
My grandpa was buried in his shoes long ago
and my sister locks the door to the bathroom. Through the keyhole
I have watched her take off her clothes
and caress her pointy breasts.
I read her diary and know for whom
she puts on lipstick. She will leave me soon.

I was a boy just yesterday.
I am the ghost of the house today,
growing up languid as a hothouse flower,
or a lizard daydreaming of becoming a dragon.

I know why my father grabs his gun
and runs up to the roof whenever the red
police light shines through my aquarium.
He never notices that I have taken out the bullets.

I know why my mother leaves at midnight,
picked up by a black limousine.
If I told her I pricked holes in her condoms
she still wouldn't know how I need her at home.

Sometimes I sit in the bathroom for hours
and imagine having a shower.

They say it happens to everybody.
But it happens now only to me.

The Sleepwalker Talks to the Curtains

Who wakes me when the sun kisses the frost?
Who dares force my blind seagulls to skate on the frozen sea?
I fear someone may find the reading glasses I've lost,

and use them to read me.
Like a quince that smells of autumn,
my dark pillow smells of me.

Who dares to call the morning light if stars still fall
in my little Queendom in the corner of the sky?
I am still the Queen
who chews her own chocolate army.
Soldiers' eyes are sugar cherries in my crown
that shines like a star.

Who dares open the curtains between newspaper headlines
and dream in my homeland in the shape of a balloon,
where untold questions bloom like mushrooms in the dark?

I meet millions of fugitive shoes
on my way to the night.
Hundreds of empty gloves become butterfly nets
chasing postage stamps
flown from the envelopes of those who read stars.

I ask only of curtains that they guard me from the light—
there is nothing here for those who live
where passersby wish each other
sweet dreams and good night.

Happy Days in the Mental Institution

The nurse comes with pills and a glass of water.
Her sharp collar cuts the air in half.
On the left lie those who pretend to be ill
to avoid execution.
On the right lie those who pretend to be ill
because they were chosen to execute those
on the left.

The patients on neither side talk,
disgusted with each other;
they gnaw pillows, piss on the floor
and fart in front of the doctor.

Whenever the nurse loudly concludes that some patient
must be feeling better
they shout from the other side that his condition is even worse,
that the patient is closer to a flower pot
than a suicide bomber.

But after midnight
when the moonlight moves the barbed wire
up the wall
all the patients
play chess so nobody wins
and punish those who feel better
with a double dose of pills.

Outside of the hospital it's worse.

Making Love

He hugs her the way an octopus grips its victim
and he whispers words in the polite tone of a desk clerk.
In the tart wine smell of their sweat
he listens to their bodies speak
'...mine...mine...mine...' —
words that slice the air and screech
like a can opener.

The scream of a swan issues
from her emerald skin, and it seems
to her that she has been here before,
on the same bed her mother was born.

A rooster scream spills from his throat
and it seems he's tossing coins into a jukebox,
into a pond, into a town whose name escapes him.

Seagulls arrive bearing the scent of burnt wings
which they gently deposit on the bed—
that burning lake
in which the moon's reflection suffocates. That same moon
that until yesterday shone so temptingly.

I wonder how many stars leave their heartbeats in pillows,
in those two sailboats with perforated floors
which will soon sink
to the bottom of the lake,
where for centuries
indifferent fish have gnawed on silence.

He kisses her the way a temple kisses its pilgrims
and she kisses him back the way pilgrims kiss their temple,
heart beating in the pit of her stomach where
only a lousy signpost remains.

He tells her that he loves her,
awkwardly moving lips plastered with chewing gum.
He tells her that he loves her
in the voice of the priest pleading forgiveness as he hangs his
    underwear
on the door of the orphanage.
He bribes her with the voice of the angel perched on his forsaken
    cloak,
seeking to trade it in, not for money,
but for children's tears.

She repeats that she loves him
until her words begin to echo,
like the evening prayers of her mother,
who goes out at dawn to pick up the preacher's underwear
on which a frozen angel sits,
to iron them and return them to the nearest church.

He caresses her skin the way he caresses the window
beyond which the fog has already swallowed the morning,
the skin on her neck, the sweat in the shape of a heart.

He kisses her gently, kissing his own hands
that have now grown to the size
of her breasts.
His palm slides further down toward her belly
to where the minefield begins.
Where fear
fashions silver crewel-work out of barbed wire.

I witnessed everything.
I watched them all night.
I lived there, hidden behind clumsily drawn curtains,
peeping through the window
into my neighbour's apartment,
trying to learn about love
through somebody else's eyes.

This Morning I Saw God

This morning I saw God
enter a concentration camp
with a raven on his shoulder.
Beneath his arm he carried
a Bible wrapped in the pages
of the morning paper.
He was fixing his hair
in the reflection of his own palm
and laughing the way optometrists laugh
in front of canvases.
He was chewing on his lacquered nails
and yelling at the soldiers
who forgot to take down
the frozen memorial plate
from the walls of the crematorium.

I almost didn't recognize him.
Escorted by a necrophilic angel,
with a gas mask for a pet,
he walked along a thorny fence
stroking his steel moustache.
To happy devils he offered bottles
of perfume in exchange
for common workboots.

Along the way, he made the sign
of the cross over the roofs of houses
which subsequently collapsed.
He smiled shamelessly,
handing out scented soaps
to prostitutes, and pointing the way
to dry bathhouses.
They deterred him by showing him their palms
with never-ending lifelines.

It was sad to see him that way: like a laid-off postman who still
wears
his uniform with pride.

Even worse,
he looked like me who was looking at him,
holding a pen, trying to figure out
why these lines I write
resemble even less what I want to say.

Changing Direction

I woke last night in my grandfather's skin.
He was shouting from the family tree, begging his razor blade
to grant him one last drop of blood, that he might win
his wager against time. I was just his maid.

Then I torched the house. A white stork's burning wings
shadowed the light of the moon as she melted away.
Go to hell, family albums; dissolve the invisible strings
that tie me to the sky. Earth is where I'll stay.

My mother was cursing me. The next minute she was gone.
My father aimed a gun at me, but the bullets were missing.
Flushed with joy, I rushed to feed each family icon
to the flames, with my kisses for a blessing.

Final Madness

Goodbye, India, my little road to final madness.
Goodbye, old sky tattooed on my soles with invisible ink
drained from twenty-year-old eyes.
It seems my shadow walked over me after
I stopped for a moment at the crossroads, waiting
for the traffic light to change.
I can still feel the bruises.

I console myself that I have imagination and will find a way
to touch the things I don't wish to understand:
a gravedigger groping beneath the skirt
of a pregnant woman,
or a swarm of devils laughing atop a traffic sign.

But with too many holes in their gloves,
and too little powder on their skin,
my generation dies beside cold railway station stoves.

They fall, those gloomy sunflowers, into hacked casks
while I weigh the shadow of my home.

Goodbye to the empty diary pages
that howl every time I take up my pen
to describe the scent of strawberries in my long hair
sold to the barber to make me a wig.
The moment that made me rich made me poorer: for a brief period
    I was indifferent
to the nuances of one eye or another.

I lie down in the rye grass in which I see bread
and listen to nurses wiping the prints
of my forefinger from the calendar.
I feel polar dogs in my room
but then I know it's just my imagination,
and that I don't have to explain.

Goodbye final madness. My generation of coffins went to India,
passed into fields of burning poppies,
while I, ashamed, mulled what I would tell them
should they one day decide to return.

Facing the TV

Please turn off that TV and listen to my silence
howling from atop the shining antenna.
Submerged in that box of colours you won't see
my old slippers jumping through the window on their way
to marry the air singing behind the garbage truck.

Look at my grey face and smell
the gasoline in the linen of my wedding suit.
Note the dust from places I've never been
kissing my trouser leg.
Touch my skin burned by hundreds of suns
concealed in books I have yet to read.

Focused on the TV screen,
you won't hear the car keys
jingle in my pyjama pocket,
nor the magic sound of night's finger tapping on the door.

Please turn off that TV and watch me vomit
the morning headlines,
with my hand already on the doorknob.
Think for a moment how fragile my state is
as I leave the house walking backward,
trying to shake off the door key glued to my hand.

Behind the wallpaper in our parlour
for years I whispered gunpowder lullabies
that only our neighbours could hear.

Only the paperboy and the postman will remember
the rhyme between us that used to sound like an anthem.

So please put down the remote and avert your gaze
from that box replaying yesterday's faces,
while I make believe I am leaving the house.
Before we begin to appear
as other people see us.

AN ORDINARY MAN

My Accent

for Višnja

I love my accent, I love that wild sea
which attacks my weak tongue.
It doesn't reside in the morning radio news
as much as in the rustle of job offer flyers
stapled to street poles.
In my accent you can find my past,
the different me who still talks with imagined fish
in a glass of water.

My grandfather was a fisherman
and I grew up on a dock
waiting for him to come back.
He built a gigantic aquarium when I was born
and every time he brought a fish
he named it immediately by some word I had to learn
until the next came... next came... next came.
I remember the first two were called "I am"
and after that the beauty of language came to me
through shining scales.
I learned watching the aquarium
and recognizing the words by silent colours.
After returning home
my grandfather would spend whole nights
making sentences by combining the fishes
who would pass each other.
It's how I learned to speak.

I left the house the day my grandfather went
fishing for a black fish he was missing
and never came back.

Now I am sitting in my empty room
as in an aquarium
talking with the ghosts of fish
I used to recognize as words,

talking with the shadows floating
over the flyers ripped off street poles.

"I love my accent...
I love my accent..."
I repeat it again and again
so as not to ask myself:

Who am I now?
Am I real or just the black fish
my grandfather failed to catch?

An Ordinary Man

I am an ordinary man with ears of ordinary silk
and I speak only with a voice I've heard somewhere,
a voice like an echo.
I've given up blunders:
that leg of mine intact in the sky
was an ordinary crutch made of rosewood
and when I talk about flowers
my voice smells of earth
in which blind moles delve.

I've given up blunders.
I know that rifle ranges,
crowded at night with sad people,
were invented only because of a law
designed to protect somebody
from my gunpowder dreams.

I admit I sometimes cry at night,
but so do the others.

I've met many people and they all resembled me.
Some hid in the breathing bodies that were already corpses,
others hid in corpses in which
an attentive ear can catch a breath.
But they all had obedient eyes. And they liked dogs.
I've entered rooms filled with snow,
I've sniffed empty bedclothes and imagined
black stockings removed from maiden legs
only for me.
But so did the others.

Sometimes from the window I notice breadcrumbs
in the hair of women I once loved.
But they are now someone else's women
and that is someone else's bread.

I am an ordinary man and it's clear to me:
whenever I was born I'll die young.
I die every day and I am no longer afraid
when in passing I notice my pale face
going by the other way.

Only sometimes
I am sad and begin to cry,
though I don't know why.
And I feel sorry I am crying
and sorry I don't know why.

But so do the others.

Gardens

Candle wax dropped from Laura's eyes
when I told her I was leaving.
Heavy as a gravestone I walked
through her cactus garden. Should I
have kissed her prayer book before I left?
I don't know yet.

Have a coffee before you go,
Elisabeth said and offered
a cold second-hand mug. Liver spots
crawled from her hand to my hand like moths
on a dead pigeon as I kissed the soil
in her garden, where plastic roses bloomed.
Should I have kissed the ten-year-old calendar
hanging on her kitchen wall?
I am not sure.

Rosemary was too young to love me
and too old to recognize her child
in my face. After leaving my ashes
in a dead volcano that resembled
an unused diaper, I left
through the back door where overgrown nettles
let me pass, telling me they needed someone
to trim them. Should I have kissed
each leaf before leaving?
I still wonder.

Winter is coming. The time when cold flakes
look for their homeland in Laura's cactus garden,
Elisabeth's plastic roses,
over the standing nettles,
and I ask what I did wrong,
searching for the hand
that will put a fresh flower on my grave.

I Married a Young Woman

She chose not to grow up watching herself
in my old eyes.
I chose to never grow old
in the eyes of my friends.
She knew perfectly well
that winter will come soon with an axe to cut down
a tree like me
who notices the weather change
watching firewood flame.
My pillow full of sawdust was invaded easily.
The rustle of new leaves made my bed sing
a lullaby for the swollen carpenter's hands.
I denied hundreds of characters who left my bookshelves
leaving the books smelling like a freshly cut tree
not ready to marry printing ink yet.
Now I am left to watch at the window,
scars on my shoulders
in place of my old paper wings.
And to wonder
if I lived in books too long
to hear clearly another calendar leaf falling down
and screaming the same way
the characters of my favourite books
laugh at me
as they head for the forest.

Angels

Angels hover over the city that eats its own roads,
whose people vanish on trains. Can you hear them?
They are not the angels we know from cards,
they don't resemble sleepy children anymore.

I am talking about angels at home in police files,
angels like flies, buzzing around computers.
I swear I caught one trying to rip out my passport photo.
Another rewrote the prescription for my glasses.
I wonder less and less about the difference
between what I remember and what I see,
why I so often find feathers in my wallet
and holes in my pockets.

Angels hover; stardust falls from their wings, covering
bed frames made from Santa's sleigh,
pyjamas that smell of graveyard soil.
They bribe the morning light to look like a TV screen
and our heads become so heavy
we understand nothing but weather reports.

They no longer live among bright clouds
and don't waste time coaxing the wind to lift
schoolgirls' skirts for fun
or decorate trees with the hats of passersby.
No more does Cupid sport with arrows,
no more are yesterday's lovers today's parents.
Angels live now among the greasy clouds,
counting the disillusionments of tardy workers.
They are too busy designing uniforms
to notice the bootprints of soldiers that remain behind.

Who knows whether a postman will recognize our fear
when he comes near our famished mailbox?
Who knows whether a policeman on night shift
will recognize the sorrow tattooed on our hands

while waving to a flock of geese leaving town?
Will a lumberjack ever understand our tears
when he cuts down the apple tree that long produced
nothing but flowers?

Yes, angels hover over the city,
disguised in the white coats of doctors
who hide their nicotine fingers.

Their fingers kiss our skin the way spiders
kiss the strings of the guitar we left in the basement
and never learned to play. Can you hear them laughing
while writing their names on the letters we send ourselves?

Old Man Waiting for the Lost Letter

for Natasha

I'm still waiting for the letter, still waiting for the autopsy report,
hoping I'm the page in your life that hasn't yet been read.
A shadow army of your lovers teases me that I'll never move forth
from the long line of spiders chewing a broken net.

I still wait for that lost letter. The last postman walks into the sky.
Snow is falling. Rain is falling. Postage stamps fall into the sea.
Letters fall from above and I wonder why
your dead lovers get letters, but there's no mail for me.

The Hotel at the Crossroads Watches the Street Musician

While dropping the warm room key
into the concierge's hungry hand,
I hear you joke about cockroaches
chewing your wallet at night,
about mice in your pocket and spiders
playing loudly with coins in your guitar case.

I know you have to open the front door
with your back before facing
that morning light heavy as a rock
on a street where people don't care
if you walk lamely or proud, but mind
if you sleep on the sidewalk.

I can read from the dirt under your nails,
from your royal fingers fishing
for the right tune in a land of patient strings
that you hit the rocket launch site,
imagining yourself in a cockpit
on your way to the moon
and that you still roam.

I am not just mortar and brick.
Just the shadow of an umbrella
that eats those who lost the roadmap
to the place that smells like home.

I am a nest for travellers, for those
who move back and forth. Grown
on the heart of the crossroads, I was home
to those coming from the West,
for those going South or East,
those heading North. Gypsy songs,
Venetian lovers, Viennese gamblers, British smiles,
Turkish hashish, Russian vodka,
Parisian perfumes, Armenian bread,

Vatican preachers, Sephardic silences,
lonely mothers, lost children:
they are my phantom family.

Listening to coins jingle
in your shallow well, I could spend
a hundred years telling you what I have seen,
what horrible secrets I hide.
I would propose to your voice,
but marry your ears, make you believe
your past was the groom and my present
the bride. I could bribe you
with the choice to be a happy ghost
or one of hundreds who hit the doorframe
walking backward to the street.
I have seen your kind of people ringing the bell
to wake up the sleepy concierge.
Some of them come back.
Some of them sleep in a better hotel.

New Telephone Number

Goodbye, old address book, my little bible,
my silent country of fingerprints.
Don't forget me, give me a call.

Ignoring the book's binding of rotten crosses,
I counted all those numbers in the dying pages.
Simple mathematics taught me
that if I divided the total by two,
I would find that I lived for ages just a few metres
away from my friends
who never picked up the phone.

And that is why I have lived all my life
in an address book.

Watching a Woman Cry in My Favourite Bar

What are you doing on this drunken ship, with sailors in a doomed ward?
Do you listen to our smoky breath, a choir of crows singing an old song?
I watched for years the wall you watch, and found only the painted board
that makes me think this ghostly place is the grave where I belong.

Your legs stretch from a tiny skirt, your blouse bravely fights your left
        breast,
makes mirrors think we should go on shaving until we sting.
Nobody notices the moment when your tears fall into the nest
of your slim finger, the white band of a missing wedding ring.

Since you divorced your beauty from us, we are knights on one horse.
We use tablecloths as shields and billiard cues as spears.
You slew our greed kissing that wall, your tears killed me sans remorse
as I stole the memory of a wedding to buy another beer.

I watch you leave your empty glass and a tip in the shape of a smile.
Another pint will finish me off before old punks become my brothers.
Soon you'll be forgotten. Regulars will put you in a gossip file.
Not me. Just thinking of you, I become better than the others.

Candle of the North

Take me to the beach, my darling,
let us walk over pebbles that don't smell of fish from the market,
walk where a breeze lazily leafs through last year's newspapers,
through decomposed documents of long-dead blood donors.

Take me to the beach
and keep in mind that I'm scared
watching children and emigrants cross the unlit street.
I no longer care to hide in my pocket
fingers red with the pain
of turning the radio dial all night,
looking for a program that plays silence.
I am not ashamed of trying to think nothing.

Perhaps we might still see that hole in the sky
from which I cut a constellation and gave it to you,
thinking it would fit in your wallet.
Last Sunday I found the same stars in the basement
hiding amongst old horoscopes and clippings
about lucky lottery winners.

Take me to the beach
and walk with me over crossword-puzzle magazines
and let us listen to those crying children who are not my own
and let me just smile to people
who smile like me.

My hands are as cold as TV news, my skin blue
as the stamp on a birth certificate.

But somewhere in a northern room
a strange candle burns and wakes me up,
a candle that I melt down,
and I smell soil when diving in my dream
to the bottom of the ocean,
looking for something promised to me
when I was born.

My hunting gun hangs on the wall
next to the photo of the deer
I followed into the minefield.
Every time I dream I walk to the stars
I find socks full of blood in the morning.

I know that East is easy,
that West is always opposite
and in the North lost people
sit around a single candle
to warm their cold fingers.
It is where mothers make sandwiches
already eaten by sorrow and the long wait
for better days.

For years I couldn't wash the breadcrumbs from my hands.
Were these crumbs from the school bags of northern children?
Those same children who need to recognize when they go home
the difference between streetlights and a wolf's shining eyes?

They are not breadcrumbs, I console myself,
they are just black sand falling from that place
from which I cut the constellation.
But I know this is not the truth.
I once tattooed a lamb on my forehead
but when I woke the next day
only bones remained.

So take me to the beach my darling,
where every single pebble has its own rhyme,
nothing but a rhyme, with no meaning.

I Am Not The One

I am not the one who wakes up with Jelena on his arm.
I just imagine the sharp sound of her boots echoing
in the empty mailbox that ate my army cheque,
tick, tock, tick, tock
toward the exit door.

I am not even the other one,
the one who will pretend to sleep and pray in sleep
that she will not forget her underwear while dressing
and spill the ashtray full of butts signed with her red lipstick,
the one who happily listens to her leaving,
tick, tock, tick, tock
toward the exit door.

I am the other one,
the one who will await the sunrise in the sound of her boots
going down to our basement apartment,
tick, tock, tick, tock
toward our bed,

the one who will pretend that the chirping of the first sparrows
doesn't sound like her tears dropping on my shoulder
while she tells me she will never get drunk again
at the party for disabled soldiers.

I am the other one
who will leave on her side of the bed new underwear
and a bird-food bag and money for a taxi
if she feels the need to find me on the beach
trying to persuade hungry seagulls to teach me how to fly.

If she finds me there in the company of lifeguards
fighting with all manner of birds attacking me,
she will understand the meaning of the silence
every time I walk down the beach steps,
tick, tick, tick, tick,
toward the exit door.

If I Told You

Would you let me slide my hand into your pants
to caress your pubic hair if I told you I am dying?
Wrapped in black foil,
carrying in the womb my own history as an illness,
I begin to resemble the wardrobe I wear.

Would you let my cold fingers play under your blouse
while speeding toward the wrong-way traffic sign
on the road that goes to nowhere?
The road is closed to my tribe.
I pass along my worries to the morning light.
Will the bed beneath your husband pretend
that the scars on your back don't resemble mine
after just the scent of orange peel remains in the grove?
Just a few seeds in the basket of the night.

If I had only told you I was dying of an unknown illness,

that I am closely watched by frozen doctors,
funeral-home clerks,
my death certificate in an envelope ready to kiss the stamp—
would you stay?

I found my question leaking from the rear-view mirror
driving you back to your home where only your wedding ring
will remind you of the forbidden rhyme

between two bodies soaked in gasoline,
two shadows that, like a burning lamp, shine.

Breath on the window that will last as long as my sweat,
the deep riverbed in the map of my palms,
the little strawberry in the handful of bitter pills
to let me live my obituary one more day
in your question:
Is this man someone I met?

The Immigrant Talks to the Slot Machine

The moment I find my winning hopes in your golden eyes
I pretend I am somebody else.
The one who married my past to dreams of a new life
but still a stowaway in the womb of a sinking boat,
I discovered I was just a daydreamer
awkwardly disguised in the shape of work gloves
soft as the skin of my future wife.

For the first time I met your eyes at the airport.
You were a luggage inspector
watching carefully for any sign of storm in my sweat.
You, my ghost protector, were measuring
newcomers' tears and their pain
against the weight of gold.
I should have known my starving suitcase was my ID,
my one-way ticket, my uniform,
that I should hide my lucky charm,
my old house key hanging on a shoelace around my neck.
Never meant to be sold.

I see your fingerprints on my paycheque,
smell your seductive perfume in the suffocating subway train.
Before I met you in my hungry lunchbox
you made my wrinkles your bed.
I planted soil in my work clothes' pockets,
waiting in vain
for cactus blooms with the pallor of my skin
that used to be red.

I still don't know what to do with my love.
My work mornings live to be buried
on Saturday night. In Sunday shame.
With Monday I hope
I'll meet your face on the screen

telling me that you still love me.
Even if you were married
a million times to those whose keys on shoelaces sway
like empty luggage carried by hand.

You wander down the airport hall
to persuade those with slim cases that you're free.

Confession of the Pimp's Cat

He makes me feel every flea
that bites me has a royal background
each time he scoops food into my precious bowl.
He's the man whose breath sounds
like a hot breeze in my February fur,
like the wind clothed by my little flag
every time he pours water in my empty dish.
My master seems the only one who pays respect
to my distant past as a leopard.

I adore his tough finger caressing
my neck under the collar bearing his name.
He respects every single life I spent
waiting for him to adopt me,
only me, from among hundreds
of simple cats who believed
there is no difference between men.
They know the difference now.

If I learn that language of seductive silence
that inhabits his eyes
every time he comes home
with his head covered with bandages,
instead of watching my own little life
reflected in two shiny bowls
I would purr a gentle lullaby
to his tattooed muscles,
to the goblins that frame his scars,
to the blood under his nails.

But I decide to learn nothing,
lying under the bed,
still wondering
if I would give one of my remaining lives
to my master
if something happened to him.

Winning Horse

My winning black racehorse got so depressed
with my white horse's habit of running only to place
that he decided to commit suicide.
He ate his own winning photos from the stable wall.
He chewed whole my glorious stud book
and died in front of the white horse,
who watched him expire with no sign of surprise.

Before my tears dried and the last breath left his nostrils
I asked the veterinarian
to transplant the black horse's winning heart
into the white horse's body.
Before the winning heart started sucking new blood,
I added kidneys and a liver to be sure
all my past went in the right direction.

I gained a fortune after my white horse went back on the track.

Sometimes I spend entire nights in the stable
where no winning photos are mounted anymore
and regret that it took me so many years
to realize that horses are as they are
and I am as I am.

The Gypsy Sings to the Policeman's Shadow

I am the hunter. I am also the trophy.
The last time I fired the rifle the wounded moon was howling
and the deer came to me asking for my armband as a collar.

Every village knows me as a dark angel and a punk,
a womanizer and a boozer and a howl unready
for the first morning light.
Yes, I am a lonely sinner,
having early morning dinner.
I watch the sky through the empty bottle of brandy
in the early morning when the light gets dark.
It's too late,
too late to learn,
because I am already drunk.

I'm sorry, shadow, your highness,
that I'm lower than your sole.
Pursuit is your holy duty, it is mine to hit the road.
I am a lonely miner,
an early morning diner,
because I never found the church's shadow bigger
than my heart that pulls the trigger
when I see deer kissing my ammo.

I find religion in the Holy Barman's words,
shouting out "Last call!"
when the wounded moon starts bleeding day
instead of night.

CIRCLE

Circle

If I am different now—life's weekend visitor,
a rose that reeks of weeds,
a humble nobody, a page number in a book,
a warm refrain for the wind that blows cold—
should I question if my parents knew
that their love planted deadly seeds?
The photos of me as a baby are a lie.
I was born long ago. Already old.

No Time to Waste

When I need the ravine church to inject my pain and fears,
I kneel down faster than I walk back up the hill.
Like a donkey in a horse race I run backward, hiding black tears
from the victor whose laurel crown stinks of dill.

The man who crosses the finish line tastes his sweat bitter,
exhaling, inhaling, life written in bruises, tattooed on his skin.
Sorry I disappoint you, father. Sorry to disturb you, mother. I'm a
faker,
a false stallion racing lambs to learn what it's like to win.

The *mala fide* maths of losses don't explain my sincere need to die.
Like the last runaway horse to cross the line
I'll enter the winner's circle when dill smells like laurel,
and nobody can tell the winner from number nine.

When I Reached the Border

Everything was in bloom, even the garbage containers,
and weeds on the borderline grew out of control.
I was a mere bricklayer in an army of mute complainers,
hands weighed down with mortar, my head a broken wall.

By the time I reached the border I was already dead
and kept checking the clock to keep myself awake,
a voluntary exile, passport inked to my forehead,
repeating my date of birth, not knowing it was a mistake.

They took from me my mother's heart, and my father's tears still
  warm.
They dumped my sister's screams in a drop-off box for the poor.
All that remained of me was love, my only uniform—
bulletproof and proudly worn for those coming from the war,

for those who strove to meet history in a blaze of gold.
I have already died once. And now I'll never grow old.

Where Is My Brick

How did I lose my shining gold brick,
buried deep in my pocket,
that day I met with fellow prisoners
to celebrate the day of our release.

We, eyes crossed by bars,
wiping old tears with handkerchiefs cut from prison uniforms
and praying for justice, not even mentioning the name of God—
we meet once a year
to see how fast our past is dying.

There is no more prison. Only gates remained after we each
took a brick on our way out.

Every year we meet to expose our swollen skin
to journalists frightened that someone will die
in front of the microphone,
and we talk to those who don't know the past,
tempted to reach for the remote control.

But in the late night,
we lonely heroes far from the street lights
sit silently warming ourselves by the old fire
fearing that there is maybe among us
some bricklayer
who stole all the bricks from our pockets.

At the End of Summer

I called my father, not knowing he was already dead.
Later I was told by doctors that he was climbing a tree,
chasing a squirrel who grabbed something
from his secret box and ran away.

He was already on his way to the place where
the ringing of a telephone has the same meaning
as the sound of a running squirrel.
A telephone was ringing but nobody was home.

I learned that the average squirrel collects food all summer for the
    winter
and buries it in some secret place. And then he forgets
where he stashed all his nuts.

While listening to the ringtone
I was thinking about that summer day my father threw me out
to be my own father after catching me
trying to open his secret box.

Years later I found myself
holding my little secret box and repeating:
I am not a squirrel, I am not a squirrel,
while waiting for someone to hang up the phone.

Summer is over, summer is over,
and I am not the squirrel.
No, I am not the squirrel,
at all.

The Shadow Behind Me

Who is behind the shadow that follows me
in the middle of the night
with a face concealed in foggy fear?
Each time I pass the fading street light
the shadow gets darker and longer
than the slippery road ahead.

It breathes the way a power mower
gasps, stuck in a field of rye,
the way a hunter climbing uphill
pants with the heartbeats of a deer.
It breathes. And breathes. And breathes.
I fear to turn my head back.

If it's a she, it must be death.
This breeze kissing my neck is like the air
from the turned pages
of the picture book I grew up with.
Morning lives in her sweet perfume.
Afternoon dozes in her soft slippers.
Night shines like dewdrops in my ears.

If it's a he, it must be my guardian angel
coming off the night shift
because his work gloves smell of hothouse compost.
He's already given my name
to the flower that blooms in the dark,
as a whole life is about the fence between
a neighbour's wife
and her husband's nervous trigger finger.

Spring is Coming

Spring is coming on crutches.
Swallows nest again in the ruins
and diapers flutter merrily on a clothesline
stretched between two graveyards. Peace
caught us unprepared to admit without shame
that we survived and that we dream of gulls and the sea.
It brought restlessness to our Sunday suits and dancing shoes;
it settled in our stomachs like a disease.

Spring is coming on crutches.
Look, idle soldiers drunkenly roam the town
afraid they'll have to turn in their uniforms if they return home.
Look, they are carrying a young man from the cinema
because he couldn't bear the beauty of a happy ending.
Look, the former hundred-metre champion
sits alone at the stadium watching the shadow
of his wheelchair.
Even my neighbours don't quarrel with the same zeal.
It feels as if we woke in our underwear under a spotlight
on the stage, and we have yet to find the exit.
The peace halved us.

Spring is coming. On crutches.
The time of medals is coming,
when children from freshly whitewashed orphanages
start searching for family albums,
the time when big flags cover this landscape of horror
in which my neighbour, in the basement,
holds a child's winter glove in his hand. And weeps.

Christmas Tree Decorations

My children and I decorate the Christmas tree.
Outside the moon howls in the eyes of a hungry dog.
I have brought from the attic a box of family ornaments.
We recognize in their reflections
our own joyful faces.

The shining decoration on top is my grandfather.
From the Russian war he brought home
just the bullet in his shoulder,
and the need to be silent
when talk turned to war.
Why did he die with a smile on his face?

This other ornament is my uncle's,
a war hero who jumped from his hospital window.
The doctors said he dreamt
of bombs being thrown into his room.
When he died he had so shrivelled
we buried him in a child's coffin,
too small to display all his medals.

That next decoration is of another uncle.
He was convinced that Communists
had planted a bug in his mouth,
which was why he spoke a language
of his own invention.
He died in prison after authorities decided
his strange words were secret codes.

The next bauble belongs to my aunt.
While gathering wildflowers
with which to decorate the liberators,
she wandered into a minefield.

This decoration, here, is my brother.
He never learned to fire a rifle properly.
The last time he pulled the trigger
he shot a Christmas tree and died of sorrow.

This last small black ornament is Mother.
After surviving the concentration camp
she dedicated her life to lighting candles,
and washing family tombstones.

I stand with my children
at the foot of the tree.
There are no more decorations.
I am thinking about how nicely
the tree's trunk will burn in our stove,
as my children dream of morning
and the presents that await them.

Tomorrow we will wake up happy.

What I Saw

I saw that human feet shrink two sizes when a person dies. On the streets of Sarajevo you could see so many shoes in pools of blood. Every time I went out I tied my shoelaces so tight my feet turned blue. God, how happy I was to return home with shoes on my feet. What a pleasure to untie the laces. What a pleasure not to lie on the street without shoes on my feet.

Before I left the house my mother would check to see if I was wearing clean underwear. She claimed that it would be a shame if they carried me to a mortuary and found dirty underclothes on me. Better to go to a blue sky with blue feet than with no shoes.

What a shame for our family, she'd say. To be killed without dignity. God forbid!

The Mathematics of Genocide

After my father peacefully died in his chair
and shrank to the size of a boy,
instead of mourning I went to Srebrenica
to search for a poem about the genocide in 1995:
8,000 men were slaughtered.
Their mothers grow moustaches.

What I found was that 87 forensic experts and 22 miners
worked 14 years to locate and dig up
the remaining 6,042 male bodies.

Officials believe they were buried
in 23 surrounding forests surrounded by 62 minefields.
The UN's File 328/03 reports claims
that bodies were dumped in cement mixers
and then spread on the soil of 23 soccer fields
to fertilize the grass.
No game is scheduled because the soccer players claim
they hear screams instead of cheers from the crowd.
Heavy rain slows the work of investigators
who wait for the government's reply
to Appeal File 1/03 asking for the exact number
of cement mixers in use at the time.

Simple mathematics tell me
that if I multiply 8,000 executed men
with an average height of 170 centimetres
it would come to 13,600 square metres,
almost the same size as Srebrenica.

Before taking the flight back
I spent the day walking to the epicentre of that circle of the dead
and found a devastated ordinary house
with a burnt-out chair in front.

I sat on it and couldn't hear even my own heartbeats.
Only the crying silence
in the dying battery of a calculator
made me feel small as a boy
waiting for his father to return.

A Short Note About Killing and Memories

When doctors didn't make our bad memories fade
my brother and I went hunting
with no guns, but with hearts hot for revenge.
Bare hands tattooed only with the date of our release
from the prison camp
were the only arms we needed.

When the cold night grew quiet as a lullaby
we were already sitting in the boat
in the middle of the river on the invisible border between
the burned Croatian fields and our burned-out country.
We doomed Bosnians were waiting
for the deer who would swim
all the way to our side seeking fresh grass,
with no care for borders.
All we had to do was catch the deer by the antlers,
push him under the water
and wait until he drowned.

We got one.
While wrestling with him we could hear him scream
and we heard his death rattle under the water
but didn't care about the millions of bugs
that swarmed the deer's thrashing antlers
and crawled up our sleeves.

We rejoiced on our bank,
we danced before the empty eyes of the deer
reflecting nothing but the wood fire
and the pot of boiling water.
We sang prison songs about escape and repeated
our old belief that enemy blood heals all wounds
when peace starts looking like counterfeit currency.

But before we reached for the knives
to consummate our victory,

thousands of bugs started biting us.
Before the pain grew unbearable and morning found
us scratching each other and dancing around the deer
we threw our clothing in the fire.
Then we shaved our bodies bare
and listened to the flames
eating our proud, growing hair.

While walking naked through the city
I heard someone tell his wife
that he had thought the era of prison camps had ended.
We smiled bitterly.

My brother said we should have called a doctor
and I was wondering
how to find his telephone number.
He said the number was the one
tattooed on our naked wrists.

We walked, watching the sunset
through the eyes of the dead deer.

The Poet and His Brother the General on a Hill After the War

We met on a hill of a summer night
where crickets played in the ashes
we used to call home.

He,
with a tiny hole in his chest I made with my pen,
me,
with scars on my skin left by his medals
hanging in place of my heart.

We promised not to talk about the end of the war
curled in his stomach
like a dead baby waiting to be reborn,
not to talk about my shaking fingers
and the fact that everything I wrote,
I wrote in the soil with my nails.

Look at that wild rosebush
growing from the corner that used to be your room!
A viper coils
on the last remaining plank of your bookcase!
Sparrows drink from the sconce on the wall
under the black frame housing the family icon.
No one can read from the record sleeve
what music we listened to
when we learned how to dance.

When the night became dark like the words we spoke softly,
we talked about astral power and our lives too small
to compare with eternity.

Lying on soft grass that had already chewed
generations of bones
we watched the sky and listened
to the stars laughing at the vain moon
who never understood
how dull he would be with no sun.

Look at the North Star that guides you!
There's your sign of Libra! Soon will appear
the Morning Star showing us home.

What's that red star flying across the sky? I asked.

It's an airplane carrying bones from the forensic centre
to be buried in a country that hasn't known war.

Then we awoke
and went downhill by different paths,
without saying goodbye.

The Soldier Sings an Anthem to the Cactus Flower

Obedient, sober, mute as a number,
I speak the sharp tongue of the shiny sword.
Nameless, fearless, tough, and cold
I live in the house set on fire.

Blood my favourite drink,
combat my word,
sorrow my faithful follower,
death my constant admirer.

A flag may change its colour or fabric,
a country may change its form.
Blueprints of hope
bear the print of my boots.

When I face the mirror
I see only a brand new uniform.
Like the flower in the crystal vase
I bloom without roots.

Every anthem rhymes
with the shadow beneath the vulture's wings.
There, history books grow like weeds
in the compost of fairy tales.

Who am I? Almost nobody!
The one faithful to my master, attached to the strings.
Just the hand, nylon line, fishing rod, seeking a golden fish
in an ocean of whales.

But when the barrack gets cold at night,
old pyjamas to new dreams married,
I lay my head on my holster and weep,
thinking of my runaway wife.

Does she still love me? Her ghost is my worst enemy.
Why does she resist being buried
under my helmet, a pile of medals, a soldier's song
to celebrate her death as my life?

Before the New War Comes

Every Sunday we play war games
to prepare for when the new war comes.
We know it's a fake. Our bloodthirsty imagination
has the shape of water pistols.

White-ribbon soldiers guard the slaughterhouse gate
where cattle humbly enter to see for the last time
their faces in the mirrors of the knives.

My red-ribbon soldiers guard the back,
where cattle leave the slaughterhouse
in little packages, like Christmas presents,
to be loaded in trucks big enough to hold an army.

Sometimes we attack white-ribbon soldiers
and spray them with red.
Sometimes they attack us
and spray us with white.
Then we count how many uniforms
need to be dry cleaned.

After stupid Sunday evening gets tired of us,
we brave future soldiers go to the slaughterhouse cantina
to celebrate with butchers our readiness to stand guard.
Over juicy steaks we sing our anthem
despite our diluted blood.

Then we go home to tell bedtime battle stories to our kids
about how free and happy cattle attack them,
before Monday knocks on our guarded doors.

ACKNOWLEDGEMENTS

This is a painful book I consider my private poetry donation to the English language. It has been written in English to gauge how much, as a poet, I feel comfortable with the language I learned by reading and listening. And how much I sound like myself. In writing this book I borrowed a few poems, already written in English, previously published in *Immigrant Blues* (Brick Books) and *From Sarajevo with Sorrow* (Biblioasis). A few lines and poems have been taken from the libretto for the opera *Differences in Demolitions* which I wrote for the Scottish composer Nigel Osborne. A few poems from my previous works and ideas, rearranged and redefined, function perfectly in their English language suits. The documentary film *When You Die as a Cat* helped me to hear how poetry sounds and my regards go to the film director Zoran Maslić. Without the help of my old friend and poet Fraser Sutherland, the rhymes in the book would sound like an unwanted pregnancy. A deep bow and hats off to my brother Novica. Just to make mention of the names of the friends, people, publishers, magazines and my pets would require another book as long as this.

My hugs go to the young poet Natasha Nuhanović (the Snowlady) for sharing her life, love and poetry with someone who died a long time ago in Sarajevo.

I thank publisher Dan Wells for waiting on this manuscript for four years. In that period of time Dan complained because I was late, I complained back for being pushed. It was a period of private suffering resulting from my being married to poetry for thirty-five years while never considering poetry as a career. Poet Zach Wells, as editor, deserves my compliments as the bridge between the book and myself.

ABOUT THE AUTHOR

PHOTO BY DIXON

Goran Simić was born in Bosnia-Herzegovina in 1952. He emigrated to Canada in 1996 under the auspices of PEN Canada and has remain an active PEN member. In addition to his own publications, his poetry has appeared in *Scanning the Century* (Penguin, 2000), *Banned Poetry* (Index of Censorship, 1997), and in numerous anthologies in Canada and the former Yugoslavia. In 2006, he founded the literary publishing house Luna Publications. He lives and works in Toronto and is currently Writer-in-Residence at the University of Edmonton. (www.goransimic.com)

Québec, Canada

2011

Printed on Silva Enviro 100% post-consumer EcoLogo certified paper, processed chlorine free and manufactured using biogas energy.